P9-CFI-688

TEEN
RIO

10/14/13

Riordan, Rick

Percy Jackson & the Olympians:
Book 3: The Titan's Curse
INDIE COMICS

DISCARD

GRAPHIC NOVEL

OCT 1 4 2013

191

FAIRPORT PUBLIC LIBRARY
1 Village Landing
Fairport, NY 14450

OCT 14 2013 191

PERCY JACKSON & THE OLYMPIANS
BOOK THREE

THE TITAN'S CURSE
The Graphic Novel

by
RICK RIORDAN

Adapted by
Robert Venditti

Art by
Attila Futaki

Color by
Gregory Guilhaumond

Lettering by
Chris Dickey

DISNEP·HYPERION BOOKS
New York

FAIRPORT PUBLIC LIBRARY
1 VILLAGE LANDING
FAIRPORT, NY 14450

WESTOVER MILITARY ACADEMY.

BAR HARBOR, MAINE.

GRRRR... VERY WELL IF I CANNOT HAVE THE GODLINGS ALIVE, THEN I SHALL HAVE THEM DEAD!

NOT IF I HAVE SOMETHING TO SAY ABOUT IT!

RARRR!

CURSE YOU!

ANNABETH!

THAT MAGIC SALVE SHOULD DO THE TRICK.

THANKS, GROVER. IT'S FEELING BETTER ALREADY.

ARGH! TAKE THAT!

YOU SURE HAVE A BUNCH OF THOSE FIGURINES, NICO. HOW LONG HAVE YOU BEEN COLLECTING THEM?

ABOUT A YEAR. I THINK. BEFORE THAT, I WAS INTO...

I DON'T REMEMBER. THAT'S WEIRD.

HEY! DOES ZEUS REALLY HAVE LIGHTNING BOLTS THAT DO *SIX HUNDRED* DAMAGE? CAN *POSEIDON--*

--THAT'S YOUR DAD, RIGHT?

HOW DOES HE MAKE HURRICANES?

I--

PERCY JACKSON.

LADY ARTEMIS WILL SPEAK WITH THEE.

BRARY
1 VILLAGE LANDING
FAIRPORT, NY 14450

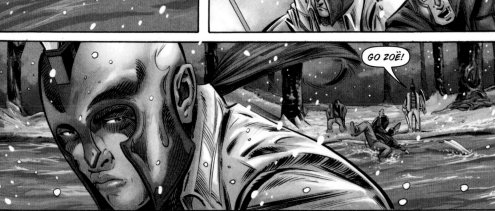

LISTEN, THERE'S A LITTLE SEA FRIEND THAT NEEDS YOUR HELP. I TOLD THE HIPPOCAMPI I'D COME GET YOU.
AGAIN?
SORRY, BOSS. WHO ELSE AM I GONNA TELL? YOU'RE THE ONLY ONE AROUND HERE THAT SPEAKS HORSE.
RIGHT. ONE OF THE PERKS OF MY DAD BEING THE GUY WHO CREATED HORSES OUT OF SEA FOAM.
I'LL BE SURE TO THANK HIM FOR *THAT* ONE.
AND DO ME A FAVOR, WILL YOU? STOP CALLING ME "BOSS."
I KNOW YOU THINK I GOT THE CENTAURS TO STORM LUKE'S SHIP LAST SUMMER AND HELP YOU GO FREE, BUT THAT WAS ALL CHIRON'S DOING. REALLY.
WHATEVER YOU SAY, BOSS. YOU'RE THE MAN. YOU'RE MY NUMBER ONE.

HERE YOU GO, BOSS. STRAIGHT DOWN ABOUT ONE HUNDRED FEET.

PERFECT. SHOULD BE NICE AND *WARM* DOWN THERE.

NATIONAL MUSEUM OF NATURAL HISTORY.

"--AND WE ARE NOT LEAVING ANYONE BEHIND."

~snort~ ~zzzzz~

YOU SHOULD BE SLEEPING LIKE THE OTHERS.

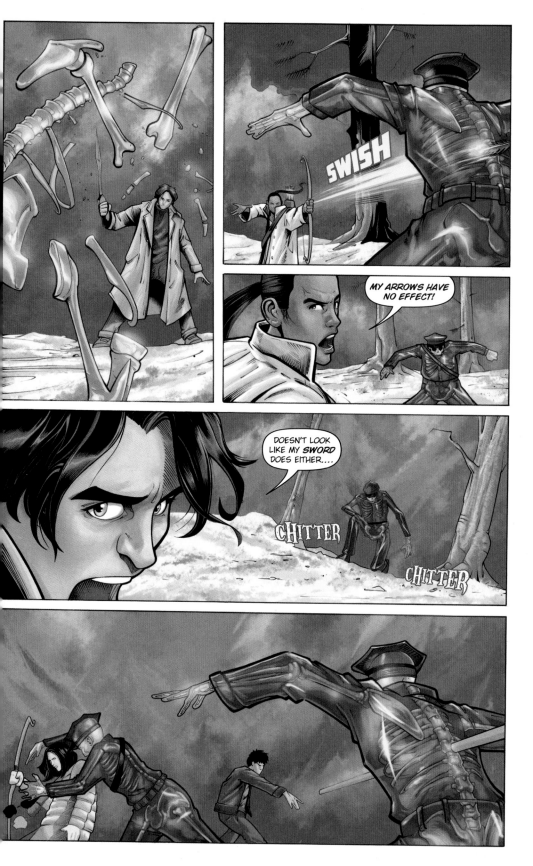

THIS IS AS FAR AS THE BOAR WILL TAKE US. WE SHOULD GET OFF WHILE IT'S DRINKING.

~slurp~
~slurp~

THANKS FOR THE LIFT, PORKY!

WHERE ARE WE?

WHEREVER WE ARE, I *HIGHLY DOUBT* WE'LL BE ABLE TO FIND A RENTAL CAR.

GUYS? WHAT ARE *THOSE*?

WE ARE ON THE EDGE OF ONE OF *HEPHAESTUS'S JUNKYARDS*. IT IS WHERE HE DISCARDS ALL HIS FAILED MACHINES AND INVENTIONS.

AND THE PATH TO ARTEMIS LEADS STRAIGHT THROUGH IT.

I DO NOT LIKE THIS. LET US REST UNTIL NIGHTFALL. WE WILL CROSS THE JUNKYARD AT NIGHT WHEN IT IS COOLER.

AND WHEN WE WILL BE LESS EASY TO DETECT.

~gulp~

BIANCA, THAT HOTEL YOU STAYED AT. WAS IT POSSIBLY CALLED--

--THE *LOTUS HOTEL AND CASINO*?

YEAH. WHY?

OH, *GREAT....*

A COUPLE OF YEARS AGO, GROVER, ANNABETH, AND I GOT TRAPPED THERE. IT'S DESIGNED SO YOU NEVER WANT TO LEAVE.

THE LOTUS MAKES TIME SPEED UP, TOO. WE THOUGHT WE WERE ONLY THERE FOR AN HOUR, BUT WHEN WE WENT OUTSIDE, *FIVE DAYS* HAD GONE BY.

BIANCA, WHO IS THE PRESIDENT OF THE UNITED STATES RIGHT NOW?

FRANKLIN ROOSEVELT. WHY...?

NO. THAT WAS OVER *SEVENTY YEARS* AGO.

DO YOU REMEMBER ANYTHING ELSE ABOUT BEFORE YOU STAYED THERE? MAYBE SOMETHING ABOUT YOUR PARENTS?

YOU GUYS ARE FREAKING ME OUT. LET'S JUST *GO.*

TIME
TO GO!

PLUNK

WHACK

WHUNK

THIS
WAY!

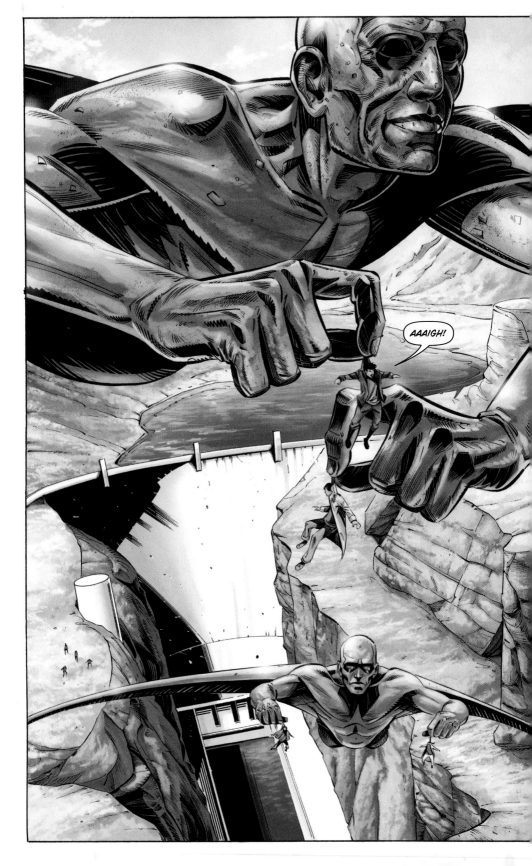

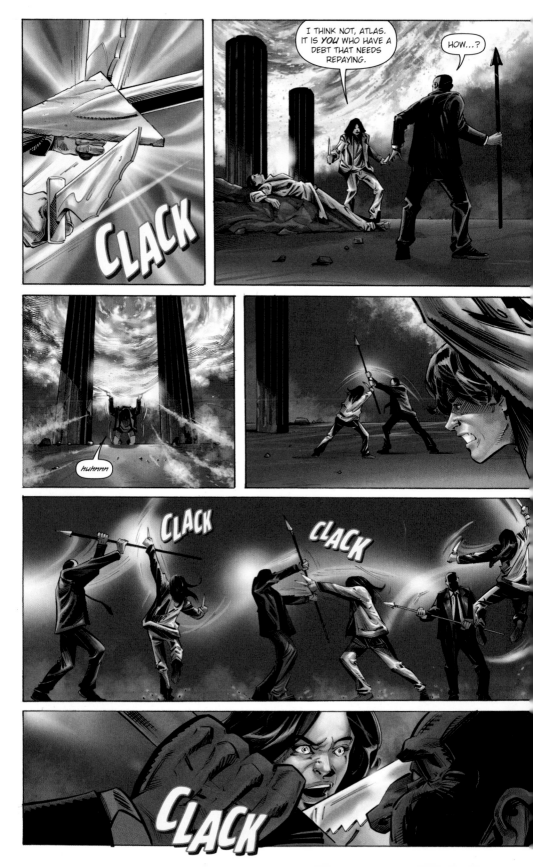

"LET THE TRIUMPH CELEBRATION BEGIN."

YOU, UH, OKAY THERE, G-MAN?

S-SURE.

I'M JUST GOING TO KEEP D-DRINKING THESE TRIPLE ESPRESSO LATTES UNTIL I GET ANOTHER SIGN F-FROM PAN....

YOU WON'T LET ME DOWN, I HOPE.

I'LL J-JUST BE G-G-GOING.

THANKS FOR STICKING UP FOR ME, DAD. I WON'T LET YOU DOWN. I PROMISE.

LUKE ONCE PROMISED HIS FATHER THAT. HE WAS HERMES'S PRIDE AND JOY. JUST BEAR THAT IN MIND, PERCY. EVEN THE BRAVEST CAN FALL.

LUKE FELL *PRETTY HARD*, ALL RIGHT. RIGHT OFF THE TOP OF MOUNT OTHRYS. HE'S DEAD.

NO, HE IS NOT.

LUKE SAILS WITH HIS SHIP FROM SAN FRANCISCO EVEN NOW. HE WILL RETREAT AND REGROUP BEFORE ASSAULTING YOU AGAIN.

I DON'T KNOW HOW HE SURVIVED, BUT HE IS MORE DANGEROUS THAN EVER. AND THE GOLDEN COFFIN IS STILL WITH HIM, *KRONOS* STILL GAINING STRENGTH.

YOU DID WELL, MY SON, BUT YOUR ROLE IN THIS IS NOT YET RESOLVED. PREPARE YOURSELF. CONTINUE YOUR TRAINING, AND I KNOW YOU WILL MAKE ME PROUD.

YOUR FATHER TAKES A GREAT RISK, YOU KNOW. WISE COUNSEL IS NOT ALWAYS POPULAR, BUT I SPOKE THE TRUTH.

YOU *ARE* DANGEROUS.

FIRST, YOUR MOTHER WAS TAKEN FROM YOU. THEN, YOUR BEST FRIEND, GROVER.

NOW MY DAUGHTER. IN EACH CASE, YOUR LOVED ONES HAVE BEEN USED TO LURE YOU INTO KRONOS'S TRAPS.

THE CROOKED ONE KNOWS HOW TO STUDY HIS ENEMIES. HE KNOWS YOUR *FATAL FLAW*, EVEN IF YOU DO NOT. AND HE WILL CONTINUE TO USE IT AGAINST YOU.

YOUR FATAL FLAW IS *PERSONAL LOYALTY*.

TO SAVE A FRIEND, YOU WOULD SACRIFICE THE WORLD. IN A HERO OF THE PROPHECY, THAT IS A VERY DANGEROUS THING.

IF HELPING THE PEOPLE YOU CARE ABOUT IS A FLAW, THEN YOU'RE GUILTY OF IT, TOO.

AFTER ALL, *YOU* WERE THE PARK RANGER AT THE HOOVER DAM, RIGHT?

THEN DON'T WORRY ABOUT ME, MOM. I LIKE HIM BETTER THAN GABE ALREADY.

I'LL SEE YOU FOR CHRISTMAS?

ABSOLUTELY! THERE WILL BE *EXTRA CANDY* IN YOUR STOCKING THIS YEAR, TOO.

I'LL MAKE SURE OF IT.

AND PERCY? THANK YOU.

OKAY, MOM. SEE YOU SOON.

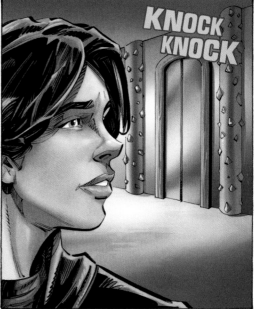

KNOCK KNOCK

HEY! ~huff huff~ I HEARD YOU WERE BACK. WHERE'S BIANCA? I WANT TO HEAR ALL ABOUT HER *ADVENTURE!*

NICO, WE NEED TO TALK....

END OF
BOOK 3.

Adapted from the novel
Percy Jackson & the Olympians, Book Three: *The Titan's Curse*

Text copyright © 2013 by Rick Riordan
Illustrations copyright © 2013 Disney Enterprises, Inc.

All rights reserved. Published by Disney • Hyperion Books, an imprint of Disney Book Group.
No part of this book may be reproduced or transmitted in any form or by any means, electronic
or mechanical, including photocopying, recording, or by any information storage and retrieval
system, without written permission from the publisher. For information address Disney •
Hyperion Books, 125 West End Avenue, New York, New York 10023.

Design by Jim Titus

Printed in the United States of America
V381-8386-5-13196
First Edition
10 9 8 7 6 5 4 3 2 1

Library of Congress Cataloging-in-Publication Data
The Titan's curse : the graphic novel / by Rick Riordan ; adapted by Robert Venditti ;
art by Attila Futaki ; lettering by Chris Dickey.—1st ed.
    p. cm.— (Percy Jackson & the Olympians ; bk. 3)
"Adapted from the novel Percy Jackson & the Olympians, Book Three: The Titan's Curse"—T.p. verso.
    Summary: When the goddess Artemis disappears while hunting a rare, ancient monster, a group of her
followers joins Percy and his friends in an attempt to find and rescue her before the winter solstice, when
her influence is needed to sway the Olympian Council regarding the war with the Titans.
    ISBN 978-1-4231-4530-1 (hardcover)—ISBN 978-1-4231-4551-6 (paperback)
    1. Graphic novels. [1. Graphic novels. 2. Mythology, Greek—Fiction. 3. Artemis (Greek deity)—Fiction
4. Animals, Mythical—Fiction. 5. Monsters—Fiction. 6. Titans (Mythology)—Fiction. 7. Riordan, Rick.
Titan's curse—Adaptations.] I. Futaki, Attila, ill. II. Riordan, Rick. Titan's curse. III. Title.
    PZ7.7.V48Ti 2013
    741.5'973—dc23   2012007895

Visit www.PercyJacksonBooks.com
and www.disneyhyperionbooks.com

SUSTAINABLE   Certified Chain of Custod
FORESTRY   At Least 20% Certified Forest Co
INITIATIVE   www.sfiprogram.org
               SFI-00993

For Text C